THE TRIAL
A NOVEL

JEN BRYANT

ALFRED A. KNOPF
NEW YORK

For Eileen and Jerry S., and for David K.

THIS IS A BORZOI BOOK PUBLISHED BY ALFRED A. KNOPF

Text copyright © 2004 by Jennifer Bryant
Jacket and interior illustrations copyright © 2004 by Leigh Wells
All rights reserved under International and Pan-American Copyright Conventions.
Published in the United States of America by Alfred A. Knopf, an imprint of Random
House Children's Books, a division of Random House, Inc., New York, and simultaneously
in Canada by Random House of Canada Limited, Toronto.
Distributed by Random House, Inc., New York.

KNOPF, BORZOI BOOKS, and the colophon are registered trademarks of Random House, Inc.

www.randomhouse.com/kids

Library of Congress Cataloging-in-Publication Data
Bryant, Jennifer.
The trial / by Jen Bryant ; illustrated by Leigh Wells.
p. cm.
SUMMARY: Living in Flemington, New Jersey, in 1935, twelve-year-old Katie Leigh Flynn
describes, in a series of poems, the effect on her small town of the ongoing trial of Bruno
Hauptmann for the kidnapping and murder of Charles Lindbergh's baby son.
ISBN 0-375-82752-8 (trade) — ISBN 0-375-92752-2 (lib. bdg.)
1. Lindbergh, Charles A. (Charles Augustus), 1902–1974—Trials, litigation, etc.—
Juvenile fiction. [1. Lindbergh, Charles A. (Charles Augustus), 1902–1974—Trials,
litigation, etc.—Fiction. 2. Trials (Kidnapping)—Fiction. 3. Flemington (N.J.)—
History—20th century—Fiction.] I. Wells, Leigh, ill. II. Title.
PZ7.B8393Tr 2004
[Fic]—dc21
2003047441

Printed in the United States of America
February 2004
10 9 8 7 6 5 4 3 2 1
First Edition

"We shall not cease from exploration

And the end of all our exploring

Will be to arrive where we started

And know the place for the first time."

—T. S. Eliot

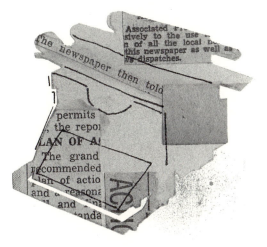

Part I

"Anne, they have stolen our baby."

—Charles Lindbergh to his wife,
March 1, 1932

"Have 50.000 $ redy 25 000 $ in
20 $ bills 1.5000 $ in 10$ bills and
10000 $ in 5 $ bills. After 2–4 days
we will inform you were to deliver
the Mony.
We warn you for making
anyding public or for notify the Police
the child is in gute care . . ."

—from the ransom note left by
the Lindbergh baby's kidnapper(s)

FLEMINGTON

I've lived in this town my whole life,
and I can tell you . . .
nothing ever happens.

Each week, the farmers bring their chickens and eggs to market
and the grain trucks dump and load up
at Miller's Feed Store on North Main.
The streets are wide and clean,
the shopkeepers are friendly,
and all the children walk to school.

At Christmas, Santa comes to the bank and gives out
candy-stuffed stockings, and on Halloween
there's a big parade at the courthouse
with cider and doughnuts
and prizes for the Prettiest, Funniest, and Scariest.

With all this, you'd think I'd be happy as a clam here in Flemington,
and why that's not so
I may never really know—

but I *do* know that whenever I read
National Geographic or *Time*
or look through one of my uncle's travel books—
the ones with pictures of glaciers and deserts,
palm-treed islands and busy cities—
I'm always wishing myself
into them.

"You're restless, Katie Leigh, just like your father was"
is Mother's explanation, but since
he left us so long ago,
I guess that's another thing
I'll never really know.

THE PHOTOGRAPH

From the photograph, we don't
look a lot alike:
his hair dark brown
(mine is black),
his eyes hazel gray
(mine are dusky green),
his nose long and thin
(mine is small and wide, a few scattered freckles
along each side),

but then . . .
there's that full lower lip
(I have that)
and his dimpled chin
(I have that too)
and the way his head tilts just a little to the left,
like he's about to ask a question
or trying to get a different perspective
(Mother says I do this all the time).

I guess I believe he's a part of me,
though I wish I had more
than a five-by-seven photo
to prove it.

AT THE RAILYARD

Sometimes I watch the train men turn the engine,
watch the boxcars unhitch and recouple,
watch the forklifts load the flatbeds
and the fireman shovel coal.

Sometimes I try to remember my father.

Sometimes, when there's nothing else to do,
I stay all day until the last train leaves,
and all I can see is a thin line of steam,
way off in the distance.

SULLEN

At the tracks, I usually find Mike, his back against
the big wooden box
where the stationmaster keeps his rain cape
and his tools.

We don't talk much.
But once in a while, we talk
a lot.
Mike told me his mother died when he was five and his father
has been drinking too much
ever since.

On sunny days, I bring a book and read it while he
whittles oak sticks into animals
with his pocketknife,
or with his hands shapes faces from
pieces of clay.

When I bring leftovers from the kitchen,
he tries to refuse, but when I
start chewing, he does too.

He borrows my books, and I know
he's smart because
he asks me all these questions
about the characters
that I never thought about before,

and I have to go home and think on them
before I can answer.

Mike is not like
the other boys I know . . . he's not
stuck-up or loudmouthed or silly.

At school, he's real quiet. He sits
in the back row so no one will notice
if he falls asleep
from staying up late waiting
for his father.

The teachers all say he's "sullen,"
but if you tell him a good joke, he laughs
the kind of laugh that makes you join in,
makes you forget
your troubles.

Once, when he walked me home,
he stopped before the big blue house on the corner
to watch the family inside at supper:
the mother serving the soup, the father
carving the bread, the children chattering—
the neat white plates,
the yellow curtains on the windows,
the warm steam rising
from the bowls.

WHEN SOMETHING HAPPENED . . .

Actually, something *did* happen here
about two years ago—
not in our town exactly, but just
ten miles away, in Hopewell, New Jersey.

Something happened
on March 1, 1932, between 7:30 and 10 P.M.,
at the home of Colonel Charles Lindbergh,
the first man to fly across the Atlantic Ocean
alone,
our bravest and greatest pilot, an American hero.

Something happened
on that stormy night,
as the wind howled outside his house on Sourland Mountain,
while the Colonel and Mrs. Lindbergh
were reading and sipping tea
and Wahgoosh, their terrier, lay curled at their feet.

Something happened
to their little baby—Charles Lindbergh, Jr., just 20 months old—
while he was sleeping in his upstairs room,
while the butler was polishing silver
and the maid was doing dishes.

Someone climbed
into a second-floor window
and pulled Little Charlie out of his crib
and carried him outside to a ladder
and climbed down holding him
while the wind groaned and a car waited.

Someone kidnapped
Charles Lindbergh's firstborn son, leaving only
some muddy footprints,
a broken ladder,
and a ransom note.

And no one saw
who did it.

MOTHER

My mother was once a dancer. She performed
in a professional company that traveled all over the country,
and once they even went
to Mexico.

She says it wasn't all
that great because they lived on a bus
and only had their costumes and one
bag of clothes and the food
was awful.

She says her life is much better
with a house and a steady job
as the assistant manager at the Union Hotel,
especially now—when so many folks
are hungry and can't find work.

But sometimes, when she doesn't think I'm looking,
I've seen her studying the world map that hangs in the den,
or staring at a beach scene in a painting,
and I've noticed how she takes an extra long time
to dust my desk where I keep my magazines,
and sometimes I find
a *National Geographic* open on the kitchen counter,

and I think that life on the road
wasn't so bad
after all.

MONTHLY RECKONING

At the end of every month, Mother sits
at the kitchen table
and does the bills.
She usually makes me leave the house
or gives me chores upstairs
so I don't hear her when
she curses.

I know she worries about money.
I know she doesn't think it's right that so many kids these days
go to work instead of school
so their families can buy food.

Last month, the Union Hotel wasn't doing so well,
and she thought there'd be a cut
in her pay.

Now business has picked up
and she knows we'll get by for a while,
"at least until April."

So that's good, I guess.
We should be fine for a while.
Until April.
At least.

THE DEMOCRAT

My mother's younger brother is
a reporter for the *Democrat,*
the biggest newspaper in Hunterdon County.

Uncle Jeff doesn't worry about losing his job,
even in these hard times.
He says, "People need news, Kay-dee,
almost as much as they need food.
And even if they can't find work,
and have to stand in a soup line,
and can't afford to buy new shoes,
and don't have money for the movies,
for just two cents a day
they can lose themselves inside black and white
and forget their troubles."

The first time he took me to the newsroom,
he was fresh out of school and working as a proofreader
for the editor, Mr. Griffin.
I guess I was hooked from the moment
I sat at Uncle Jeff's desk
and tapped my name on the typewriter
and filled his notepad with scribbles
and watched a reporter make a story from a chaos of notes
and watched the printing press spit out
the next day's headlines
and smelled the ink on the rollers

and saw the trucks roll up to take the papers to every
newsstand and street corner for miles around.

That was four years ago.
Uncle Jeff's moved up to reporter, and has his own byline
on the front page almost every day.
Mr. Griffin says he has *instincts:* "Like a bloodhound . . .
he sniffs out a story when no one else can."

At first, Mr. Griffin didn't like me visiting.
"Girls talk too much," he grumbled.
But then he saw how I wasn't in the way,
and how I helped find spelling mistakes
(I even found one in a headline)
and would run copy to the printers,
and when he asked me for a synonym for "argue" and I
gave him seven without stopping for a breath,
he started calling me "Word Girl."

Now, whenever I'm there,
he shows me the front-page layout
and lets me help in the darkroom, developing pictures.
He has a big voice that scares me sometimes.
His desk is a mess, and his cigars
make my eyes water,
but he loves that *Democrat,* loves
the words and the smell of ink and the electricity in the room
when there's a good story and only
a half hour until deadline. Someday, I think I'll work
for someone just like him.

OBSESSED

Mother has given up trying to make me
decorate my room like a normal girl.
On the wall above my bed, I've stuck up with thumbtacks
a dozen *Time* magazine covers
and a collage with headlines from the *New York Times:*

"GANG MURDERS PUZZLE POLICE"

"LINDBERGH SETS NEW SPEED RECORD"

"PROHIBITION REPEALED—LIQUOR LEGAL AGAIN!"

"ROOSEVELT TO ADDRESS THE NATION: MILLIONS WILL LISTEN AND HOPE"

"DUST STORMS RUIN CROPS IN MIDWEST—FAMILIES DESTITUTE"

"SEARCH CONTINUES FOR BABY'S KIDNAPPER"

Taped to my closet door
are all the postcards I've collected
and my own handwritten descriptions
of the pictures.

Sometimes, when I'm bored, I rearrange them
while Mother stands cross-armed, her back against my door.
"Obsessed" is what she calls me.
Once, I heard her tell our neighbor
that I'm making up for the fact that I don't
have a father.

That's when I told her:
I'm going to be a reporter for *Time* and maybe the first

woman to interview the guards at Buckingham Palace
and to walk the whole length of the Great Wall of China,
and I plan to live for a year
among the Masai tribesmen of Africa,
who grow seven feet tall and drink blood from the necks of cows,
and I'll photograph the mountain folk of Ecuador,
who raise llamas and worship the sun.

I showed her the scrapbook she gave me for my birthday
and how I'd filled it with ideas for news stories
and how I'd pasted my own captions on the photographs
and how I could arrange them just so
and set up the text in different kinds of print
so you'd know what's important
and what you can skip.

When I was finished,
she sat quietly and looked at me
like she was seeing me for the first time,
as if I were this strange kid just dropped into her house
and not the one, these dozen years,
she'd raised and fed.

"Katie Leigh Flynn, I believe you," she said.

THE SEARCH

In my scrapbook I've kept
all the news articles and photographs I can find
about Colonel Lindbergh
and the kidnapping of his son.

If you said
that this is another of my obsessions,
I'd have to say you are right.
After all, when you live in a town where
nothing much happens
but chickens, eggs, and Santa Claus,
then you'd better pay attention
when something does.

According to my clippings,
a few days after the baby was taken,
someone sent a ransom note to Colonel Lindbergh
demanding money,
demanding a meeting,
demanding "no police."

Someone named Dr. Condon,
who had read about the baby in the papers,
offered to act as Lindbergh's messenger,
and agreed to meet the kidnapper
late at night
in a cemetery in New York City.

Someone who called himself "John"
took the ransom ($50,000 in police-coded gold notes)
from Dr. Condon, late at night
in the cemetery in New York City,
and in a heavy foreign accent told him
Little Charlie was alive and well
on a boat called the *Nelly*
near Martha's Vineyard, Massachusetts.

But when Colonel Lindbergh went there,
he found no one:
no boat named *Nelly,* no more notes,
and no baby son.
Nothing.

A few weeks later,
a day laborer in Hopewell
walked into the woods to relieve himself
and stumbled upon a little body, half buried,
long dead.
The Lindbergh baby.

It's been more than two years since then
and the police have still not found
who kidnapped Little Charlie,
who killed him and left him in the woods.

Since then, the newspapers have printed
hundreds of articles
about Colonel Lindbergh and his wife—
how they fly as a team to Europe, Africa, and the Far East,
how they've had another son,
how they try to give their new son
a normal life.

LITTLE PIECES

The year that Uncle Jeff hitchhiked clear
across the country, he sent me
a postcard
from almost every state. I have one from

Pennsylvania (fishing on the Susquehanna River),
Ohio,
Illinois (pretty boring—a field of corn),
Missouri (my favorite—Jesse James's hideout cave),
Kansas,
Colorado (canyons and the river),
Utah (the Great Salt Lake),
Nevada,
California (two guys beside a giant redwood),

and when my friend Mary Beth moved to Wisconsin,
she sent me a lumpy one
with a cow on the front, and when you
squeeze, it says "MOOO!"

My great-uncle Eamon in Dublin sent me one
of a medieval castle on a hill
where two knights fought to their death
for the love of an Irish lady.

Mrs. Hoffmeyer at the bakery gave me
a hand-colored card

(a little girl, dressed for a festival, in a red ruffled skirt and black boots)
that she got from her family in Germany,

and when Miss Culberry from the library became a missionary,
she sent me one of an African woman
with so much jewelry on her neck,
I wondered how it didn't break.

These cards are my little pieces of the world
and every time I look at them,
I realize how much there is outside of Flemington
I need to see.

Uncle Jeff says,
now that Colonel Lindbergh has flown across the ocean,
someday regular folks like us
will be able to fly on a plane
as easy as taking a bus.

I thought he was kidding.

But then one night I lay awake in bed
and tried to picture that in my head
and I think he might
be right.

BAR TALK

Yesterday, two policemen from Trenton
stopped at the Union Hotel
for a couple of drinks. Mother said
they were both off-duty, and they both
wanted whiskey.

Mr. Carter, the bartender,
called Mother over
just in case they started trouble,
just in case their tongues got loose.

The older one didn't talk so much,
but the younger one did:
Very recently, in New York City,
someone was spending gold-note money,
the kind the government had stopped producing two years ago,
the kind that was used
to pay the Lindbergh baby's kidnapper,
the kind the police could trace.

Federal agents were closing in
on someone in the Bronx, someone
they were sure to catch
real soon.

Tonight after dinner,
I'm putting more blank pages in my scrapbook,
just in case.

MIKE

They say:
His father was bad news
in school.

They say:
You just wait—
Mike's gonna turn out just like him.

They say:
Kids like Mike
never amount to much,
and some end up
in prison.

I say:
Have you seen him
fetch his father from
the hotel bar
when he's had too many whiskeys?

I say:
Do you see how hard he works after school
stacking boxes and cleaning floors
at Bailer's stationery store?

I say:
Were you at the tracks

when he helped
an old hobo out
from under a boxcar?

I say:
Do you see him late at night,
waiting up for his father,
doing his assignments on a milk crate
in that dingy little room
on South Main?

I say:
Mike's all right,
and someday
he'll prove you all wrong.

FIRESIDE CHAT

After dinner we listened to our President, Franklin D. Roosevelt,
who spoke to the whole nation on the radio.
He has a plan—he says it will work—
to save our economy.

The way I heard it, he's got some government projects
(building roads, planting trees, and digging ditches, for instance)
that will take:

Time
Manpower
Muscle
Sweat

but which will make
three million new jobs for Americans
so they don't have to stand in soup lines,
so they can earn an honest wage,
so they can buy warm clothes
and feed their children.

There are so many kids in this town
whose fathers
don't have work.
I hope they are listening to this.

I hope the President knows how much
those fathers need those
trees, ditches, and roads.

I hope Mr. Roosevelt is the kind of man
who does what he says, the kind
who keeps his word.

WISH

The other day I was grumbling again
that nothing exciting
ever happens in this town.
This time Uncle Jeff agreed:
"My biggest story last month was the fire
at the five-and-dime and the opening
of the new soup kitchen in Somerville . . .
but a lot of folks all over the country
are pretty bad off, Kay-dee,
so maybe we shouldn't complain."

I felt guilty for a while about wishing for excitement
when most folks didn't have
a warm place to sleep
or food on the table
or books to read
or a job.

Then yesterday Uncle Jeff came running up our front steps,
waving the headlines.
"Hey, Kay-dee! You're gonna get your wish.
The police think they've got
the Lindbergh baby's kidnapper!
Trial's going to be at the courthouse here
in Flemington! Right after the New Year!"

I ran to tell Mother at the hotel, but first
I stopped at the Baptist church
to donate some canned food and clothing
for the children living
in shantytowns near Philadelphia,
whose faces won't make the front pages,
but whose stomachs are empty
all the same.

SLEEPLESS

I can't believe
there's really going to be
a murder trial
here in Flemington.

I'm trying hard
not to think about it too much,
I'm trying not to get
obsessed.

What if *I* were that Lindbergh baby,
snug in my crib after my nanny
tucks me in? Then—
a pair of hands, a dark sack . . .

The house is quiet. Mother's asleep.
If someone climbs to my window,
I hope they'll see
I'm too big to steal.

CHALLENGE

Last night after work, the men at the *Democrat*
challenged the men from the lumberyard
to a basketball game
outside, behind the firehouse.

Lots of folks came,
even though it was dark
and a few degrees below freezing.
The firemen aimed their headlights on the court,
and we huddled on one side, with our mittens
and mugs of hot cider,
to cheer them on.

They played pretty evenly,
with Uncle Jeff leading the scoring
for the Newsmen, and Big Hal Lowenthal
pulling down all the rebounds
for the Jacks.

At the start of the second half,
Big Hal (who weighs more than three hundred pounds)
went up for a rebound and came down
on Uncle Jeff.

Everybody laughed as Lowenthal stood up
and held out his hand.
Uncle Jeff held up
a swollen arm, the one
he broke twice in high school, the one
he'd just broken again.

PLEADING OUR CASE

Mother got suspicious
when I offered to finish the dishes and put them away
so she could rest after her long day,
and she looked at me curiously
when I picked up the magazines I'd left
scattered on the living-room floor
before she even asked.

When Uncle Jeff called to say
he was stopping by
and could he pick her up anything on the way,
she nodded like she knew
something was up.

We took turns telling her
why Uncle Jeff needed me at the trial, and why
she should let me off from school
so I could help:

"I can get extra credit in Social Studies."
  "You should let her see history being made firsthand."
"I've already read all the books on the seventh-grade reading list."
  "She'll be developing her writing skills every day."
"We could use the extra money, Mother."
  "Katie will be paid just like a regular secretary."

"All my report cards say:

'Easily bored.'

'Good intellectual potential.'

'Could use extra challenges.'"

"She'll never have another chance like this one."

Then Uncle Jeff said he hoped his injury
wouldn't keep him from covering
the biggest trial of the century,
and he sure hoped he wouldn't lose his job
if it did.

The whole time, Mother sat on the sofa,
legs tucked underneath her,
like a Far Eastern queen
hearing grievances from her subjects.

At the end, Uncle Jeff asked
if she'd be the first
to sign his cast.

Mother wrote:

To my kid brother—
You're still a smooth talker.
Get better quick.
Your loving sis, Maureen K. Flynn
P.S. I'll think about it.

DOORS

Mother doesn't believe too much
in churches: "I got married in one,
and just look what happened."

But today I slip in through the side door
of the Presbyterian church,
where we visited last Christmas, right after
Mother found me on the roof of our house,
feet dangling over the eaves like it was some fishing pier,
and even though I told her
(over and over and over I told her)
that I was simply trying to find a quiet place to think,
she was convinced
I was working up the courage
to throw myself off.

I sit way in the back and look up
at the stained-glass window
where Jesus stands with a lantern in one hand
and knocks on a big brown door
with the other.

Mother said it means
He's knocking on the door of Heaven,
but from all I've heard,
Jesus was a pretty curious guy, and I figure He and I
have a similar wish right now,
which is simply to get inside.

I figure if I meditate on that door for at least an hour
I can *will* myself into that courtroom,
but just in case,
before I leave, I'm going to kneel down
and pray a little too.

VERDICT

Mother came home early today
so she could stop by my school
and talk to the principal.

Mike and I rode our bikes
up and down Cemetery Hill until
I thought my legs would fall off.

When I walked into the kitchen, she was stirring soup
and Uncle Jeff was setting the table
with one hand, and when I
looked down at my plate, there was
a note on the back of a napkin
in Mother's neat script:

Just this once, you're excused
for six weeks or until
Jeff's arm gets better, whichever
comes first. Work hard. Have fun.
P.S. Clean your room.

Part II

"LINDBERGH KIDNAPER JAILED"

—headline of the *Daily News*,
September 21, 1934, following Hauptmann's
arrest and before any evidence was presented

ROOMS TO RENT

You would think
Flash Gordon himself
had landed in town.

There must be
three hundred reporters
and just as many radio folks
squeezing
into any empty space
they can find.

Mother says
three of her friends
are renting out rooms to WNBC News,
and two others
have taken in men
from the *Herald Tribune,*
and still another
has kicked out her own brother
so she can rent his room.

It appears
that the trial of Bruno Richard Hauptmann,
the man accused of taking the Lindbergh baby,
is good for the economy.
It appears
that because of him,
the good folks of Flemington
will make a killing.

COLONEL SCHWARZKOPF

Though his name is thoroughly
German, he's
an American, head of
the New Jersey State Police.

The newspapers say
there's been a lot of pressure on Colonel S.
to find the Lindbergh baby's kidnapper
and to bring him in.

Last night, at the Union Hotel,
Mother showed him
to a corner table,
where he waited for the Attorney General
and his wife.
The glasses clinked like sharpened knives
as they toasted
his success.

A FISCHY STORY

My uncle's old friend Will Flanagan
works for Colonel Schwarzkopf.
Today, he told Uncle Jeff what happened
when the police questioned Bruno Richard Hauptmann about the
$14,000 in gold notes they found at his house.
It went something like this:

Colonel Schwarzkopf: "Where did you get this money?"
Hauptmann: "From my friend Isidor Fisch."

Schwarzkopf: "Where did Mr. Fisch get it?"
Hauptmann: "I don't know. I didn't even know it was money."

Schwarzkopf: "What do you mean, you didn't *know* it was money?"
Hauptmann: "He gave me a shoe box wrapped in paper. He asked
            me to hold it for him while he went back to Germany."

Schwarzkopf: "So why did you open it?"
Hauptmann: "I had given him my own money to invest—a few
            thousand dollars. But he lost it in the stock market—
            all of it."

Schwarzkopf: "And then what happened?"
Hauptmann: "Fisch left for Germany. He was feeling sick. He died. I
            opened the package to see what was inside."

Schwarzkopf: "Did your wife see the package?"

Hauptmann: "*Nein.* I mean, no."

Schwarzkopf: "Did you tell her about the money?"

Hauptmann: "No. I hid it in the garage. She did not like Fisch. She did not like me investing our money."

Schwarzkopf: "So you have no idea how Fisch got the Lindbergh ransom money?"

Hauptmann: "No."

Schwarzkopf: "And only you and Fisch knew about the money?"

Hauptmann: "Yes."

Schwarzkopf: "And Fisch is dead."

Hauptmann: "Yes."

Schwarzkopf: "That's not good."

Hauptmann: "No. *Das ist nicht gut.* That is not good at all."

IMAGINE

Imagine you are Bruno Richard Hauptmann,
accused of murdering the son
of the most famous man in America.

Imagine you are Anna Hauptmann,
his trusting wife,
who works in a bakery
and takes care of her baby boy
and has no idea
how she will pay for a lawyer
to try and save her husband
from the electric chair.

Imagine you are William Randolph Hearst,
the most powerful publisher in America,
who owns newspapers and radio stations,
who stands to make millions of dollars from this case,
who already has millions to spend,
who doesn't mind paying a lawyer
to defend Bruno Richard Hauptmann
so that at least this trial will appear
fair.

Imagine you are Edward Reilly—
known in New York City as "Death House" Reilly
because you haven't won a murder case in years—
and there are rumors you're an alcoholic who chases women

instead of the truth.

Imagine you are hired to be part of the Lindbergh trial,
the biggest court case of the century—
imagine your delight.

Imagine you are David Wilentz,
the prosecuting attorney,
who must try to win a case where nobody saw anything
and all the evidence
is circumstantial.

Imagine then you learn
that Death House Reilly is the defense attorney. . . .
Imagine how confident you feel.

CEMETERY HILL

This is the closest I've ever been
to flight.

Bending low, cycling down as fast as I can go,
wind hissing in my ears, whipping my hair,
my eyes teary from the speed.
I feel completely free.

From the top you can see
the whole town spread out like a giant quilt,
each street a seam, perfectly straight,
the church steeples like compass needles,
pointing to the sky.

To my right, the fields where we play
baseball and run footraces in summer,
asleep now under snow.

To my left, the stone gates of the cemetery
where the ancestors of Flemington
watch over us.

Colonel Lindbergh scattered Little Charlie's ashes
over the Atlantic Ocean so no one
could make a spectacle
of his grave.

If the jury finds Bruno Richard Hauptmann
guilty,
he'll die in the electric chair.
But they won't bury him here.
I wonder what his grave will look like.
I wonder if anyone will care.

LINES

Overnight, it looks like some giant
spider spun her web
between the utility poles
in front of the courthouse.

There must be a hundred lines reaching across
the street, stretched out to houses and storefronts and churches,
and even to the hallway of the Union Hotel.

Every place they can find a space,
the news folks are
setting up makeshift radio stations
and sending live updates
about the trial.

I can't decide which I like better:
the old, sleepy town
or the new loud and crowded one.

I sure do miss
walking down the street
and knowing everyone I meet
and not getting shoved and pushed
in the grocery store
and not having to wait
so long for a phone line
and not having to worry

whether our town will become famous one day
for frying someone in a chair.

On the other hand,
it sure isn't boring
anymore.

UP AT JEFF'S

"That bachelor's rat hole" is what Mother calls
the two-room apartment
above the grocery store
where Uncle Jeff sleeps (and sometimes eats) and keeps

a single bed,
a small gas stove,
a lopsided table,
two chairs,
and his books.

To tell the truth, I've never seen a rat
or a roach or even a spider up there, and when I come to visit,
he lets me sit
in the one good chair
and read whatever I want.

He has 369 books (I counted them one rainy Sunday).
He doesn't have shelves.
The titles are in no particular order.

When you walk in, it looks like
someone robbed a library and dumped all of it
in huge piles—some of them taller than I am—
in the middle of the floor.

On real cold days, I like to sit by the window
with a cup of Ovaltine
and read down the spines:

The Complete Shakespeare Tragedies
Little Orphan Annie's Secret Code
The 1934 Yearbook of Astronomy
Ulysses
The Good Earth
Flash Gordon and the Monsters of Mongo
The Life of Grover Cleveland
Tarzan of the Apes

I figure if I read every book in the room
without stopping for sleep or food,
it would take me
two years, eight months, and six days.

Back in October, I asked Miss Marshall
if I could get extra credit in Math
for figuring that out—
but she said she didn't believe my uncle
had that many books,
and furthermore, she had "neither the time nor interest to verify."

When I told my uncle, he had a
photographer from the newspaper
take a picture of his room and sent it
to red-lipped Miss Marshall
with an invitation to dinner. She never
came over for a meal, but I got
that extra credit.

NEW YEAR

Mimi Connelly threw a party
for all us kids
in her father's furniture store. We played
musical chairs in the
living-room section, then
sat down to
lemonade and cake
at a cloth-draped kitchen table
with a tag that said
HALF PRICE OR BEST OFFER.

Mike was there, wearing
a new blue sweater
he'd bought with the money
from his stockroom job
at Bailer's Stationery.
He looked real nice.

He sat between Mimi and me
at cake time, and I noticed
how he kept glancing outside
like he was waiting
for someone to come by.

At 11:59, we gathered around
Mr. Connelly's big blue radio
and listened to the countdown on WOR.

When the announcer cried "Happy 1935!"
we blew cardboard horns
and threw confetti while Mimi's father played
"Auld Lang Syne"
on the piano at the window.

That's when I saw Mike's father
leaving the hotel bar,
holding tight to the handrail
and stumbling through the snow.
I looked across the piano
at Mike, and he turned to look at me,
and we both said "Happy New Year"
anyhow.

SLEEPLESS AGAIN

Tomorrow is my first day
in court.
Mother made me clean my room twice
and shovel the snow
off the front steps
so I'd be tired enough to sleep.

It didn't work.

I keep getting up to check the supplies
I've organized on top of my dresser:
>   Three notepads
>   Five pencils
>   Tissues
>   Small box of cough drops
>   Pencil sharpener
>   Chewing gum
>   Press badge (KATIE LEIGH FLYNN, HUNTERDON COUNTY
>   DEMOCRAT printed in big black type)

Mother made Uncle Jeff promise
to take a picture of me
wearing my press badge and holding my notes
like I'm some kindergartner on my
first day of school.
He promised he would, even though I
kicked him hard under the table.

I can't tell if I'm scared or nervous or just
excited, but whatever it is, I can't
sleep a wink wondering about what
Bruno Richard Hauptmann
might look like in person
(tall, big-boned, maybe a scar somewhere)
and how close we'll get to Charles Lindbergh,
or if we'll sit next to anyone
famous or filthy rich.

The flakes are falling harder
against my window, and as I
climb back under the sheets,
I hear geese sweeping through the black night,
urging each other on
with their common song.

INSIDE

It feels a little like church on Christmas Day:
the wooden benches are hard,
and we're packed in tight as typewriter keys
on a portable L.C. Smith.

Like a preacher, Judge Trenchard sits up front,
high above us,
and the jury's corralled like a chorus
behind a banister
that Mr. Wilentz slides his hand across
when he talks.

The ceiling must be thirty feet high,
and there are five big windows on either side
where you can look out and see
the weather and the crazy web of telegraph wires
crisscrossing the street.

The witnesses sit in a plain kitchen chair,
and the lawyers and their helpers
sit behind a long rectangular table, pens
and notepads ready.

If you count all of the
guards
court reporters
secretaries

journalists
lawyers' assistants
spectators
telegraph operators

there are almost five hundred of us
in this space made for only
half that many.

My stomach feels fluttery and my back aches already,
but I don't care—
I think about that day I prayed in back of the church,
and I wonder if Jesus is still knocking
on that big brown door,
asking to come inside.

THE JURY

2	farmers
1	railroad man
4	housewives
1	insurance salesman
1	educational advisor
1	retired carpenter
1	bookkeeper
1	machinist

By day, they will sit in court
and listen.
At night, they will eat and sleep
across the street,
at the Union Hotel.

Four women.
Eight men.
One dozen Hunterdon County citizens
chosen to decide
whether Bruno Richard Hauptmann
will live,
or die.

JUDGE TRENCHARD

I swear he played Santa Claus
three years ago
in the lobby of our bank.
All the papers say he's
seventy-one, well respected, and as
serious as they come.

But I've seen him somewhere before,
and I'm pretty sure when I was nine
he was wearing red and white
and handing out candy canes to little kids,
making his lists and
checking them twice.

Mother says it's my imagination
running wild again.

Still, something inside me wants to
run up to Judge Trenchard,
plop on his lap, and tell him
how good I've been.

CHARLES LINDBERGH
ENTERS THE COURTROOM

Tall.

Very tall.

Handsome (like my father in his picture).

Plain gray suit, black shoes.

Quiet.

Cautious.

Very cautious.

Pistol strapped to his shoulder.

Sits beside Colonel Schwarzkopf.

Does not speak.

Does not fidget or look around.

A lone island in this swirling sea

of reporters, lawyers, celebrities, gossip hounds.

Tall.

Quiet.

Cautious.

Lonely.

Lindy.

HERO

Flying brought him fame
and fortune, brought him attention—
the good kind and the bad.

From all I've read about him,
I know he's a private person—quiet and almost
shy. Likes to be
alone to think, like me.

I wonder what it's like for him now
with no more quiet evenings to read
or to tinker with engines,
no more long walks
along avenues lined with trees, just thinking
and listening to street sounds
and birdsong.

He still flies a lot, but
crowds wait at each landing strip,
and at every coffee shop and restaurant,
pushing and shoving, craning their necks
to get a glimpse.
They watch his every move.

The clouds are his only refuge
from flashbulbs and notepads,
from autograph-seekers
and sleeve-grabbers,
from the constant responsibility of being
Charles Augustus Lindbergh,
American hero.

THE DEFENDANT

I was expecting someone
older
and meaner
and uglier
and, well, more like criminals
are supposed to look—
more like the movies.

Bruno Richard Hauptmann is not
tall
or ugly
or handsome
or fat
or muscular
or scarred.

He looks like Mr. Hughes,
my fourth-grade teacher,
and a little like Mr. Loreen,
who runs the gas station
on the corner of North Main.

He looks pretty normal, pretty much
like the rest of us.
Except,
each day after court, we go back
to our homes and our families and friends,
and he goes back
to jail.

THE LADDER

Today, we heard
from a wood expert, Arthur Koehler,
and though the defense lawyers claim there's no
such thing as an "expert on wood,"
we listened
to every word he said:

The ladder
was built in three sections,
each part sliding neatly
into the next,
like a telescope,
so it was easy to carry.

The ladder
was left behind
at the scene of the crime,
and later found
by the police.

The ladder
was made of wood
from a lumberyard
in the Bronx, New York,
not far from
Bruno Richard Hauptmann's house.

The ladder
was fashioned from different sorts
of planks and boards,
and one of them
probably came
from the attic
of Hauptmann's house.

The ladder
had a broken rail,
which was why
the kidnapper slipped
and probably dropped
the baby, the poor
little half-asleep baby,
who probably
died instantly.

SOUVENIRS

Outside the courthouse
you can buy a miniature ladder
for a dime,
or two for nineteen cents.

At the newsstand
someone is selling autographed pictures
of Lucky Lindy.
Funny—no two signatures
look the same.

A boy on the corner screams:
"Get your GEN—YEW—WINE piece
of the Lindbergh baby's hair!
Blond and curly! Hurry! Hurry!"

Mother says there's a waitress named Claire
who works at the bar,
who used to have long blond hair,
who decided just this week
to walk down to the Main Street Barber Shop
to get it chopped off.

WITHOUT A DOUBT

I got a letter from my second cousin Susan,
who lives in New York.

Dear Katie,

Last week, when we went to see
Tarzan and Flash Gordon,
the theater also showed a newsreel
of the Flemington trial.

You are so very lucky
to have the Lindberghs
and all those movie stars
practically in your backyard!

My friends and I, we agreed that we'd never
seen anyone who looked—
without a doubt—
more like a baby-murderer
than Bruno Richard Hauptmann.

                    Love,
                    Your cousin,
                    Susan

        P.S. We hear they're selling
              locks of the baby's hair—
              if you can get me one,
              I'd be ever so grateful.

ANNE LINDBERGH TAKES THE STAND

I knew she'd be small.
In all the newspaper photos, she only comes up
to her husband's shoulder.

But today, she looked as though
she wished she were
invisible.

I've read a lot about Mrs. L.—
shy, a real bookworm,
a writer and a poet,
but also a

Navigator
Pilot
Loyal wife and daughter
Adventurer
Explorer
Millionaire heiress
Radio operator
Philanthropist
Mother

Of course Charles Lindbergh would choose someone
with character.
Of course he would choose someone with spirit, with brains.

Of course she would expect a long and happy life
in their country house
with their curly-haired son.

Of course.

BABY CLOTHES

Mr. Wilentz presented the tiny
gray sleeping suit
that the kidnapper sent back
to show he had the baby,

and a pale yellow shirt
found on the body
in the woods near Hopewell
in May of 1932.

Mrs. Lindbergh sat very still,
and for a minute
quietly fingered them
in her lap.

We all sat very still
for that minute until
she spoke quietly:
"Yes, they are his."

Mr. Reilly did not
cross-examine.

FINGER MUSIC

On the sidewalk next to the street,
when all the cars are done passing,
if you stand real still,
you will hear

something that sounds like
rain when it falls
hard
on a tin roof,

something that sounds like
the ends of a hundred pens
tapping fast
on a metal desk,

or maybe it's more like
the ticking of our kitchen clock
when I'm up late, waiting
for Mother.

It's the sound of news
written down, sent out
on typewriters and telegraphs
from our little town.

It's the sound of thousands of words
that will be read tomorrow

in New York, Cincinnati, Dallas,
London, Berlin, Paris.

Someday I want to sit
in some small room
in some faraway town
and make
that very same sound.

"HEY, DOCTOR!"

Those were the two words
that Colonel Lindbergh swore he heard
on April 2, 1932,
late at night
in a New York cemetery,
where he went with Dr. Condon
to deliver the money
for his baby.

"And since that night, have you heard
that voice again?" asked District Attorney Wilentz.

"Yes, I have," the Colonel replied.
"It was Hauptmann's voice."

There was so much talking and jostling going on
that Judge Trenchard had to bang his gavel
hard
and call: "Order in the court!"

I wondered how anyone could remember
  one voice
    two words
      in three years.

My uncle whispered: "We have more than
a hundred witnesses to hear, but I can't see
that any jury will dare to disagree
with Lucky Lindy."

Neither can I.

ANGELS

On Friday, when I told Mike
I hadn't been in school for a while
on account of my
writing for Uncle Jeff at the trial,
he didn't
ask a lot of dumb questions,
he didn't
ask me to buy him a souvenir,
he just
nodded and said: "I'll bet you're good at that."

He was late for work, so we kept on walking,
taking the shortcut
over the fenced-in courtyard at St. Magdelene's,
where the snow lay four inches deep
and a pair of marble angels flew
over the painted gate.
Silent, they let us through.

Part III

"Is das nicht ein ransom box?
Ja, das ist ein ransom box.
Ist das Fisch ein clever fox?
Ja, Fisch ist ein clever fox! . . .

Ist das nicht ein ransom note?
Ja, das ist ein ransom note!
Is das nicht ein *Nelly* boad?
Ja, das ist ein *Nelly* boad! . . ."

—from a song composed
during the trial that mocked
Hauptmann's German heritage

WALTER WINCHELL

Every evening after dinner,
his voice booms godlike from the speaker:
"Good evening, Mr. and Mrs. America, and all the ships at sea!"

Mother said when I was younger,
I believed Walter Winchell
lived in our radio.
She said her sides would hurt
from laughing so hard
when she watched me try
to coax him out.

Now that the great Walter Winchell,
America's best-known radio star,
has come to Flemington,
I can see for myself
how human he is.

In the courtroom, he wears
dark glasses and a fine tailored suit
and gets to sit up front, near the jury,
because he's famous.

Sometimes he even passes notes
to the lawyers.

Every night
we listen to him tell America
what's happening in Flemington,
and how he believes that Bruno Richard Hauptmann
is mighty guilty,
and how he believes
Justice will be done.

WHEN THE STARS COME OUT

It seems like Hollywood has moved
to New Jersey,
and that anyone who is someone
has come to see the trial.

This morning, just for fun, I make a list
of the famous people I see
on Main Street:

1. Jack Dempsey, the heavyweight boxing champion.
   He looks uncomfortable in a suit,
   but Uncle Jeff says it's the best disguise
   for a fighter. Hardly anyone recognizes him (but I did).

2. Ginger Rogers. She's the best dancer ever—
   even Mother says so. And she's prettier
   in person than on the screen. Unlike Mr.
   Dempsey, she *wants* to be seen.

3. Ford Madox Ford. My uncle's read all of his novels
   and thinks he's the greatest writer of our time,
   but since most folks can't afford to buy books,
   Mr. Ford's writing articles about the trial.

4. Margaret Bourke-White, the famous photographer
   and editor of *Fortune* magazine. I've never seen

anyone move so fast . . . she darts among the crowd,
flashing her camera and a smile. I hope
she publishes her pictures of our town.

5. Mrs. Ogden Livingston Mills, the New York heiress
who arrives each day in her chauffeur-driven limousine,
a pair of sleek Pekingese stretched out on the seat.
In court, she mostly yawns or reads magazines.
She must have nothing better to do.

6. Adela Rogers St. John. She's the most sought-after
New York reporter and the best-dressed woman
in town (a new suit every day—paid for by
her publisher. Uncle Jeff is jealous.).

7. Jack Benny, who has an awfully funny radio show.
He smokes the same cigars as Mr. Griffin.
I'll bet he makes more money, though.

BOXCARS

At the tracks, I used to see
boxcars filled with
cattle, chicken, sheep,
lumber, coal, steel.
Now there are still
some cars that carry cattle
to market, timber and coal
to distant towns for
building homes and burning
fuel—but lately, there is
a new kind of cargo: more
and more cars are carrying
homeless folks who are
drifting from town to
town, looking for work and
a place to live. Today,
I saw a whole family in
rags and a girl who looked
my age. I wonder if
they know who Bruno
Richard Hauptmann is—
or if they care. I wonder if
they've seen my father.
The girl waved a sad
and lonely wave as
the train rolled by,
and I've been trying all
night to erase her face
from my mind.

LOOPS AND LINES

Two handwriting experts testified
that Bruno Richard Hauptmann wrote the ransom notes
to Colonel Lindbergh.

The courtroom was quiet
as a Quaker meeting
when they posted photo enlargements
of Hauptmann's writing
next to a letter from the kidnapper.

The experts said
that almost all the loops and lines
"match those of the accused,"
and furthermore,
the same words were misspelled
again and again
and the grammatical mistakes
were all the same.

Mr. Reilly quickly pointed out
that virtually all German immigrants
whose second language is English
would make the same grammatical mistakes,
and furthermore, the police
had ordered Bruno Richard Hauptmann
to take dictation (not once but seven times!),
and include all the misspellings and grammar errors

from the kidnapper's letter,
and wouldn't let him
correct them.

Several members of the jury
yawned
and looked bored as housecats
after a full meal.

Mr. Reilly was perspiring
and was probably thinking
about his next martini.

And me, I just wrote down
exactly what they said,
exactly how they said it,
as fast as I could.

TAKING DICTATION

Have you ever held a pen
for so long
your knuckles ached?

Have you ever had to write
for (almost but not quite)
eight hours straight?

Have you ever been so afraid of missing
a single word or syllable
that you tremble
just thinking about it?

Uncle Jeff says: "Don't write every word,
just what's important."

I say: "But when a man's on trial for his life,
isn't *every* word important?"

So we worked out a system for the courtroom:
3 elbow pokes means: *Write down everything.*
2 elbow pokes means: *Just the main idea.*
1 elbow poke means: *Don't bother, take a break, look around.*

Today, after court was adjourned,
Uncle Jeff asked
if this trial work was too hard—
if maybe
I missed my school.

My look was as blank as a
fresh sheet of onionskin
as I elbowed him
once in the ribs.

DAVID WILENTZ

Whenever I look at him—
I can't help it—
I think of a hawk.

Maybe it's the way he circles the jury,
sizing them up as if
they were mice in a field.

And his voice—so shrill and precise.
Each day he hammers home
his case, telling us that Bruno Richard Hauptmann is
"Public Enemy Number One,"
a man with "ice water in his veins."

He seems awfully smart.
At New York University, he was at the top of his class
and now has "political ambitions."
I asked Uncle Jeff what that meant.
"It means he's not satisfied to be
the state's Attorney General—
he wants more, whatever that is."

I don't understand a whole lot about
power, about politics.
But I know, just by watching him in the courtroom—
finger pointed, voice raised, striding up
and down before the judge—
I know that if I were on trial for anything at all,
I would want him on my side.

BETTY GOW

Little Charlie's nursemaid, the last one
to see him
alive.
A young woman from Scotland,
devoted to her
little charge,
hysterical
when she found the crib that night
empty.
Henry Johnson, her boyfriend, questioned
extensively,
living in the U.S. illegally, deported
immediately.

Today Miss Gow told us how
she discovered Charlie was missing,
how she ran to Colonel Lindbergh,
praying he was playing
a practical joke.

His look when she asked him
where the baby was
made her blood run
cold.
Then—the frantic search through the house,
the peering into cabinets and closets,
under beds and couches,

everyone calling: Charlie, Charlie, Charlie!
The listening for his cry, but only
hearing the sound of the
wind,
    wind,
        wind,
shrieking through
the nursery window.

MILLARD'S TALE

Millard Whited is a dirt-poor farmer
who lives in the woods near Hopewell
in a shack with his two
brothers, his wife, and five kids.

When the police visited Millard's place
a few days after the Lindbergh baby was taken,
he told them:
No, he hadn't seen anyone who looked suspicious
around town.
No, he hadn't seen anyone with a car and a ladder.
No, there hadn't been a stranger
lurking in the woods nearby.

Now it seems
Millard has changed
his story.

In court, after he vowed to tell the truth,
the whole truth,
and nothing but the truth,
Millard said he'd seen a man
hiding in the bushes near the Lindberghs' home
shortly before the baby was taken.

When Mr. Wilentz asked Millard
if he could identify (without a doubt)

the man he saw hiding in the bushes,
Millard pointed to
Bruno Richard Hauptmann.

Uncle Jeff's friend at the police station
says the prosecution
offered Millard thirty-five dollars a day,
a new suit,
and all his expenses paid.

And guess what? After all that,
Millard's new suit
doesn't even fit.

JANUARY 11, 1935

She was the first woman to fly
solo
across the Atlantic Ocean, and the first to fly
solo
round-trip across the country.

Today, Amelia Earhart made the first
solo flight
from Honolulu, Hawaii, to California.

Three thousand four hundred and eight
miles in eighteen hours.

Today, in the courthouse in Flemington, New Jersey,
I sat five rows behind the first man to fly
solo
across the Atlantic Ocean in 1927.
He came home to headlines and newsreels
and ticker-tape parades,
his life forever changed.

When I look at him now,
I wonder if he wishes
he never did it.

COLLECTORS

In a file cabinet at the *Democrat,*
Mr. Griffin keeps a collection of articles
written about
Hitler.

He cuts out
columns and photographs
from magazines and big-city newspapers
and tapes them in a
spiral-bound book.

Uncle Jeff has seen it.
I haven't.
So today, I worked up the courage to ask
if I could.

I thought Mr. Griffin might be mad
(he's sort of a private person)
but instead he said: "Okay, if you'll show me
the collection you have at home."

We stayed late at the newsroom
to look through each other's books.
He gave me a Dubble Bubble cigar, and he smoked
a couple of his Tiparillos, the ones
that make my eyes water real bad.

He liked my book a lot,
especially the section I'd started long before the trial
about Colonel Lindbergh.

He called me "clairvoyant," and when I
asked him what that meant,
he said: "You can see the future."

I told him
that would sure be nice, but I didn't
believe I could.
I was just obsessed
with travel and adventure,
and Charles Lindbergh happened to do a lot
of both.

Mr. Griffin's book was filled with clippings
about Hitler
and the persecuted Jews.
There were pictures from the *Daily News,*
the Baltimore *Sun,* and even one
his friend had sent him all the way from London.

In the *New York Times,* there was a picture of
ten thousand Jews marching in the streets,
waving placards and banners.
Since the trial, I'd almost forgotten the rest of the world.
I didn't know how bad things were.
"Is there any *good* news?" I asked.

Mr. Griffin grinned, and crushed
his cigar on the corner of the desk.
"As a matter of fact, there is, Katie Leigh.
This weekend, I'm taking your mother
to the theater."

PERFUME AND CIGARS

I never even knew my mother
owned a bottle of perfume, but tonight
I got a good whiff
of "Venetian Passion,"
and it made me sneeze.

We haven't talked at all
about her going out,
and I think she's trying not to make it
a big deal. But lately
she's been humming when she does the dusting,
and suddenly she's asking me
what I think of her new hairdo and the rouge she's using
to highlight her cheeks.

When it's time for her to go,
I'm going to be curled up with my scrapbook
wishing I were in India or Timbuktu,
or someplace where only the flowers smell good
and the only smoke there is
comes from a fire in the middle of the village
where everyone gathers to tell stories,
where everyone shares.

SIGNS

There's a sign on the door that wasn't there before:
"GOOD AMERICAN-BAKED BREAD AND DESSERTS."

The old sign said: "Hoffmeyer's Bakery—Breads
and Desserts from Original German Recipes."

Mrs. Hoffmeyer has hired an English girl
to work the counter, while she stays
in the back.

Mrs. Hoffmeyer used to give me samples
of éclairs and oatmeal cookies,
and crumpets that melted in my mouth.
She taught me how
to say *"Ja"* and *"Nein,"* and *"Bitte"* and *"Danke."*
She taught me how
to count out a dozen in German.

Mrs. Hoffmeyer always gave bread
to the poor kids who'd come to the back door
and to the hoboes who knocked
after hours.

Mother says Mrs. Hoffmeyer is afraid now.
She says Germans aren't popular because of
Bruno Richard Hauptmann

and Hitler, the German Chancellor,
who hates the Jews.

I can't imagine that
Mrs. Hoffmeyer would be accused of a crime
just because she's German.

Mother shrugs.
"Everything German is suspicious these days."

If Hitler were Irish,
would Mother and I
need to hide?

POCKETS

Tonight, when Mother got off work, she looked
more tired than usual.
I made some tea while Mother put her
feet up on the table
like she does when she's too
exhausted for etiquette.

When I asked what happened, she said
two of the waiters had seen William, the new assistant chef,
stealing bread from the kitchen,
and last week they'd watched him
slip half a chicken
into the pocket of his apron.

"Best chef I've hired in five years," Mother said.
"Every day he shows up early, stays late,
and never bellyaches about the pay."

After her shift, she walked clear across town
to see where he lives
with his wife
and four little kids.

"You can't call it a house at all—he rents
a garage with broken doors and cardboard
on the windows. There's hardly any light,

and the boy who came out with no coat on
to fetch wood had an awful cough."

"You gonna fire him for stealing?" I asked.

"No. I don't think so . . .
But I think next week I'll talk to the boss
about giving William a raise. And in the meantime,
I'm going to find him an apron
with bigger pockets."

INSIDE, OUTSIDE

Today, on my way back from the *Democrat,*
after I'd helped Uncle Jeff
type up my notes,
and proofread his column,
and go over what would probably happen
tomorrow, I saw

Sarah Blake and Mary Salvucci and Mimi Connelly
setting up a display
in the front window
of Bailer's Stationery.
I stopped and tapped
on the glass, and they
waved, but they kept
working and I saw it was

a project that our
history class had made
about the Revolutionary War.
There were essays by
everyone in my class
and a shadow box with
little soldiers made from
wire and papier-mâché,
which told the story
of Washington's crossing
the Delaware to attack
the British.

For a minute, I
missed my school desk,
my spelling book, the
smell of chalk and pencils,
and even Miss Marshall's
impossible math,
her bright red lipstick
and bad breath.

Through the glass, Sarah asked:
"How are you?" and
"Is it fun being inside
at the trial?"

I nodded, but I felt
strange seeing them
rearrange those soldiers,

and me just standing there,
watching.

EXCHANGE

In exchange for her permission
to miss six weeks of school
so I can help Uncle Jeff at the trial,
Mother made me promise to put every penny I earn
as a "temporary secretary" for the *Democrat*
into the empty coffeepot in the kitchen,
the one she's labeled "Katie's Future Fund"
with her thick black pen.

If I touch it, she says she'll sell me
to a band of crazy gypsies
who have never heard
of newspapers or reporters.

I know she's kidding about the gypsy part,
but not about
saving that money.

What she doesn't know is that
I get paid fifteen dollars cash per week
and I only put ten in the pot, and the rest I put
in the cigar box under my bed,
which I've labeled "Mother's Vacation Fund"
with her thick black pen.

HOW IT IS

I don't know what
came over me.

We sat at the tracks,
watching the conductor switch engines, sipping
Ovaltine and talking about the trial.

Then Mike told me how last night
he'd had to drag his father home
again—
how he felt so full of anger,
and how sometimes he wished his father
were dead.

I told him: "At least
you *have* a father, and not
just a picture. At least
you have one to show your school papers to,
and to teach you how to throw a baseball,
and to buy you a special gift at Christmas."

Mike glared at me hard,
like Mother does
when I've really crossed her line.
"For a smart girl," he said, "you sure are
stupid about how it is."
His lower lip trembled, and I knew then

that Mike's dad didn't do any of those things,
that most days Mike didn't have
a real father either.

I felt bad about what I'd said, but I couldn't
take it back.
My mind wanted to say "I'm sorry," but my jaw
was all locked up, so I just
stood there silent as a stone and watched him
walk back home.

RICHARD BRUNO, BRUNO RICHARD

His wife says his name is Richard.
The police and all the newspapers call him
Bruno.

He's the same man: an alien, a stowaway
on a boat from Germany
after World War I, where he lived
in Saxony with his mother.

Records show he served
some jail time for a crime
he committed (a burglary in which
he used a ladder).

Richard says that after the war,
times were hard, food was scarce, and almost everyone
stole things
from time to time.

His wife says he works like a dog
for their little family,
and even though she did not approve
of the risks he took in the stock market,
and even though she did not like
Isidor Fisch,
she does not believe Richard
is a kidnapper.

Word has gotten out that Mr. Reilly
told Mrs. Hauptmann
that she should say she knew about the money
from Isidor Fisch
that her husband hid in the garage.
*"But Mr. Reilly, I did not know, so that
would be a lie."*

On the stand, Anna Hauptmann told
the truth.
She believes that honesty will keep her husband
alive.

ANNA'S ALIBI

When Anna Hauptmann
took the witness stand,
she told us where her husband was
on the night of March 1, 1932.

"My husband, Richard, who is a carpenter,
came to Fredericksen's Bakery
to drive me home.
I work there a few days per week, and on Tuesdays
I work late.
He arrived around eight.
I locked the shop,
and we went home for the rest of the night."

All the newspapers say
that Anna Hauptmann is a loving mother
and a hardworking, loyal wife.
So wouldn't she say anything?
Wouldn't she lie to save Richard's life?

TOM CONNELLY'S FURNITURE STORE

In fifth grade, we worked out a deal:
I could do my homework
at one of the big wooden desks
that Mr. Connelly displayed
in the front window,
and Mother would give his daughter, Mimi Connelly,
free dancing lessons.

I was a live advertisement for "practical home furnishings,"
and Mother knew I was just across the street
doing my assignments
while she worked at the hotel.

This was just fine until
Mimi broke her ankle on the playground
and couldn't dance for a year
and Mr. Connelly moved the desks to the back to make
room for the new piano.

Yesterday, when I stopped by to say hi,
Mr. C. showed me some new metal desks and his latest line
of living-room chairs with tags that said:
"Available in Forest Green, Eggshell, and Electric Blue."

Before I left, I got a drink from the sink in the storeroom
where the stock boys eat lunch,

and it was there I saw
one blue chair with a pair
of leather straps tacked to the back.
The tag had all the words crossed out, except
"Electric."

And underneath,
someone had scribbled:
"SOLD to Bruno Richard Hauptmann."

SNOWBALL

Someone broke
Mrs. McTavish's
dining-room window.

They did it with a
snowball
that landed on her
hand-carved mahogany table
at exactly 5:07 P.M.
yesterday.

Mrs. McTavish says
she saw someone on the sidewalk
who looked a lot like
Mike
around five o'clock.

Mike says
he wasn't anywhere near
Mrs. McTavish's, he was
across town shooting
baskets behind the firehouse.

Mrs. McTavish lives
in the biggest house
on South Main Street
and owns two cars
she doesn't even drive.

Mrs. McTavish is a member of
   the School Board,
   the Women's League,
   the Hospital Auxiliary,
   the Town Council.

No one saw Mike
shooting baskets
behind the firehouse.

Starting tomorrow,
Mike will go
straight from school
to Mrs. McTavish's
for four hours of chores.

She figures three weeks
of this routine
is fair payment for
the broken window.

It looks like
I'll be going to the tracks
by myself
for a while.

FRAMED

"I packed a rock in ice, chucked it
hard
through the old lady's window,
and ran."

That's what Bobby Fenwick said
to his best friend Leonard Frye
when I stood behind them in line
at the bakery.

I dropped
my bag of bread on the counter
and ran.

At the tracks, I was all
out of breath and hot under my coat
from running.

"Bobby Fenwick did it—
I heard him tell Lenny at the bakery.
You gotta go tell Mrs. McTavish
that it's Bobby who should do
those four hours of chores."

Mike didn't even look up
from the stick he was whittling
with a pair of broken scissors.

"I'm a drunkard's son.
You're a dancer's daughter.
Bobby Fenwick is a surgeon's son.
His mother is on
    the School Board,
    the Women's League,
    the Hospital Auxiliary,
    the Town Council.
If you were Mrs. McTavish,
who would *you* believe?"

I got mad and said:
"You can't just give up, you can't
let him get away with that. . . ."
And when Mike didn't answer,
or even move,
I stomped and fumed up and down the tracks,
like Mother does
when she's caught me fibbing.

When I came back, Mike
was still sitting real quiet
and whittling his stick,
and I decided he was probably right—
no one would believe us over Bobby Fenwick,
no one would understand
how it is.

THE IMAGE

Evening comes early, spreading
its ink over our town.
The thermometer reads twenty-five degrees.

I pull on my coat and head down Main Street, then left
onto Mine, then one block and right again
past St. Magdelene's Church
and the statue of Mary glowing in stone,
past the houses on Park Avenue
with porches and big windows.

Inside the houses, I see people laughing and talking,
children playing and mothers cleaning up after dinner.
At the corner, fire engines sleep
behind roll-up doors.

My breath fogs in front of me.
No one else is out.
It's quiet except for the *hissssss* of icy flakes
against the phone poles
and the cars tucked beside the curb.

Across the street, my feet plow a trail through the park.
Beards of ice droop from the fountain.
The gazebo squats like an old woman
in her shawl of snow.

At the far edge of the park, I stop and look up
at the third-floor window in back
of the courthouse. There's a bright yellow light,
and off to the left,
a shadow.

Could it be Bruno Richard Hauptmann?

What does he think about?
Is he cold? Is he hungry, or tired, or afraid?
Does he miss his house? His friends? His own baby son?
Would he rather be in a boxcar to nowhere?

If he's guilty, is he sorry?
If innocent, is he filled with rage?

The snow falls harder now. More ice, that steady *hissssss.*
I flop down on my back, flap
my arms and legs: open—close—open—close—open—close.

I used to make snow angels every Christmas
when I was little
to cheer up our neighbor, Mrs. Soames,
who lived alone.

Maybe tomorrow,
when Bruno Richard Hauptmann looks out,
he will see
this angel.

Part IV

"A fellow that ha[s] ice water in his veins . . . [the] filthiest and vilest snake that ever crept through the grass . . ."

—Attorney General David Wilentz,
describing Bruno Richard Hauptmann to
the jury

"Where is our conscience, where are our feelings when we have sent an innocent man to his death[?] . . ."

—defense attorney Edward Reilly,
in his closing remarks to the jury

APPETITE

Verna Snyder is a jury member
who weighs more than
250 pounds.
Verna Snyder has quite
an appetite.

Last night, Mother worked the dinner shift
for two waitresses who fell
sick with the flu.
She served supper to the jury members
in their private dining room
in the back of the hotel.

Mother said that Verna Snyder had:
15 dinner rolls
1 large steak
2 baked potatoes
2 pieces of pie
3 cups of coffee

and afterward she danced
with another juror
to the tune of "Casey Jones."

Verna Snyder made the whole
place shake,

and the jury foreman got a look on his face
like he wanted to hide.

After that, Verna Snyder
didn't feel so well,
so Mother and three other waiters
helped Verna climb the stairs
to her room.

Back in the kitchen,
the cooks played "Casey Jones" on the phonograph,
stuffed their aprons with towels,
and did the Verna Snyder shuffle
until closing time.

BULL

Once they called him the "Bull of Brooklyn."
Once they said he was one of
our country's best lawyers.

Now they call him "Death House" Reilly
because of all the cases
he's lost.

Before the trial, Mr. Reilly promised
to bring in dozens of witnesses
who could prove
that Bruno Richard Hauptmann
is innocent
and that Mr. Wilentz's arguments
are baloney.

Mr. Reilly has not kept his promise.
Instead, he's found only a few folks willing
to testify, and most of *them*
have criminal records.

He has visited Bruno Richard Hauptmann
only once, for thirty minutes,
and argues constantly with
his assistants.

In court, he often mumbles so no one can hear him,
or he shouts like we're all
five miles away,
and sometimes he forgets what he's saying
to the jury
and has to walk back
to check his notes.

I've seen his assistants try to reason with him, try
to get him to visit
Bruno Richard Hauptmann, whom they say
begs every day from his cell,
"Please, I need to see my lawyer."

But apparently, Mr. Reilly thinks he needs only
his long experience,
his fancy suit with the flower on the lapel,
and a double martini
every few hours or so
to win.

TELLING THE TRUTH

Until today, Bruno Richard Hauptmann
has remained cool,
has remained calm, and has not
shown any tendency to anger—
even when Wilentz's witnesses
pointed
    shouted
glared
    scowled
stared.

Until today, the defendant
seemed pleased with Reilly's case,
his claim that Bruno Richard Hauptmann was a
poor carpenter who was framed
by a crooked friend,
and that the Lindbergh baby
was really taken
by a whole gang of men.

Then, today, Mr. Reilly
summoned one
    unreliable
crazy
    wishy-washy
confused
    fanatical

witness after another
who claimed they saw Bruno Richard Hauptmann
on the night of the crime.

"Where is he getting these witnesses?
They're killing me!" Hauptmann exclaimed.

Everyone agreed: this time he was
telling the truth.

WHO WAS VIOLET SHARP?

She was . . .

a maid to Mrs. Morrow, Anne's mother,
and a helper to Mrs. Lindbergh whenever they visited;

a young woman who liked to dance
and to drink at the local pubs;

a pretty girl who attracted many men—
some of them honest, some of them not;

a tidy lady who kept a bottle of jewelry cleaner
(marked POISON) in her bedroom closet;

the first servant who knew that the Lindberghs
would remain home on the night of March the first,
to give the baby (he'd caught a cold) some rest;

a nervous girl who seemed shaken
when the police asked her whereabouts
on the night the baby was taken;

a desperate maid who drank
that bottle of sodium cyanide, and died.

TRUTH

Every witness so far has sworn

to tell the truth the whole truth

and nothing but the truth. Well . . .

if each one has spoken sincerely and

honestly to the best of his

or her ability then I guess

Truth must be like a mansion

with many hidden rooms or like a lizard

that's too quick to catch

and turns a different color to match

whatever rock it sits upon.

SCRIBE

Judge Trenchard has declared:
No typewriters allowed in the courtroom—
no microphones or cameras
(though we watched a New York reporter
sneak one in and hide it beside the jury).

At Bailer's stationery store, Mike
had to check in the back for more
blue and black pens,
No. 2 pencils,
and notepads,
which Uncle Jeff bought
and charged to the *Democrat*.

Before we left, I told Mike
all about the trial, and he told me
about school
(I haven't missed much).
Then he asked when I'd be back.

I said I guessed it would be at least another week
before I had to give up my job
as a *Democrat* scribe
and go back to being just plain
Katie Leigh Flynn.

NIGHTMARE

I dreamed I was walking down Main Street
with Charles A. Lindbergh
and everything was fine, everything
was quiet,
for about five minutes, until
out of nowhere there came

a crowd of
white shirts, notepads, flashbulbs—
who pushed me aside, shouting:

Mr. Lindbergh! We're here from
    the *Herald*
    the *Times*
    the *Daily Record*
    the *Sun*
    the *Recorder*
    the *Sunday News,*

and we'd just like to know
    where you'll be spending your vacation
    what you think of politics in Europe
    what your thoughts are on the trial
    what name you've chosen for your dog
    what you like to eat for breakfast
    where your mother lives (can we have her telephone number?)
    how we can reach you next week;

and furthermore, we want
>to interview your chauffeur and butler
>to follow you on your next shopping trip
>to know what soap you use
>to sit inside your plane
>to get a copy of your appointment book
>to snap a few more pictures.

Thank you so much, Mr. Lindbergh, we're so awfully sorry
to take up your time.

GUEST

On Sunday, Mr. Griffin came to dinner.

Mother curled her hair and made
pot roast, baked potatoes, and candied carrots,
the kind she only cooks
at Christmas.

It made me tense trying to be polite
when it wasn't
even a party or a holiday,
and I had to excuse myself to the living room
just to burp.

The whole meal, they kept
smiling across at each other and saying things like:
These are fine potatoes, Maureen, and
Would you care for more pot roast, Fred?
while I just sat there chewing my carrots.

Mr. Griffin ate more neatly than I thought he would,
and he didn't smoke a single cigar.
After dinner, I watched him help Mother clean up
and I got a feeling
this wasn't the last time
he'd visit.

NELLIE'S TAPROOM

For days, Mother had tried
to shoo her away, afraid
the Health Board would have a fit
if they saw a stray dog
in the Union Hotel.

But since the trial, a New York reporter
has made her his pet—
he calls her "Nellie."

Mother's boss has built a new bar
to accommodate the crowds.
He asked all the employees to come up with
a name that would sound
warm and welcoming, and not too formal.
They tried a few, like "The Town Lounge," "The Union Tap,"
and "Main Street Stop,"
but nothing stuck.

Now, each night, when all the out-of-town writers
and radio folks gather there for drinks and dinner,
Nellie noses their knees and eats
all the leftovers they feed her.
I think she knows she's found a home

and that taproom
has finally found its name.

THE QUESTION

Yesterday, before we walked the last block
    to the courthouse, Uncle Jeff asked me:
        "Do you think he's guilty?"

I laughed because I was just about
    to open my mouth and ask him
        that very same question. We sat

on a bench in front of Elsie's Shoe Palace,
    and I told him I'd been up late almost
        every night trying to sort it all out, and I

had come to believe that Bruno Richard Hauptmann
    could have been involved
        and that he surely was no angel

(he was a convicted minor thief), and I had
    come to believe too that it was possible
        that Bruno Richard Hauptmann never set foot

on the Lindbergh property, that his ex-friend
    Fisch and an accomplice (after all, the police found
        two sets of footprints on the ground)

carried that baby from his crib,
    hid the ransom, and got away clean,
        leaving Hauptmann to take the blame.

I had come to believe that there was enough
    "reasonable doubt" about this case
        that the jury should return a verdict

of "Not Guilty." I wanted Uncle Jeff,
    in the worst way, to say:
        "Katie Leigh Flynn, I believe you,"

just as my mother said that night
    I told her I wanted to be a reporter.
        But Uncle Jeff just sat there, saying nothing.

He stared down the street at all the news folks
    swarming on the courthouse like starving bees,
        and then he lit a cigar that Mr. Griffin had given him.

I sat there next to him and watched it burn.

SYSTEM

Every day, I'm writing as much as I can
as fast as I can,
my hand darting like a crab in quick bursts
of cursive,
back and forth across the page.

At the end of each session,
my fingers are so cramped
I can hardly hold the pen.

My uncle's arm is healing well.
Soon, the doctor says, he'll be able
to use his fingers. Then—

I'll have to go back to
seventh grade, back to
long division, Latin verbs, and the battles
of the Revolutionary War.

I expect my history teacher, Mr. Witkowski, will ask me
what I learned at the trial
about Law, about Criminals,
about our American Justice System.

I expect he won't be happy
with my answers.
I expect I'll have to change the subject
if I want to get an A.

MR. MITCHELL'S MAIL

At the end of our block, behind the tailor's shop,
he lives with his collie dog, Mel.

He's nearly 95 years old,
and he wobbles when he walks,
like he's on skates.
In the winter, when he forgets
to fetch his mail from the porch,
I stop and ring his bell.

At 25, he almost died
fighting at Gettysburg with General Grant.
"Turned the tide of the whole Civil War," he'll tell you,
and serve you up some soup.
He forgets a lot, but he'll never
forget that.

He wanted so badly to go
to Florida, to a big reunion
for Civil War vets.
But just last week he got a letter that said
there would be no reunion—
they couldn't raise the funds.

He shrugged, and said: *"Things are bad everywhere, I guess,"*
but I could tell he felt depressed.
This year, those ten thousand vets
will have to remember that war
alone.

PEAS AND CARROTS

Mr. Griffin came *again* for dinner.
If you saw the mess on his newsroom desk
you wouldn't believe he could eat so neatly.
He smelled like aftershave.

He told us a joke about farmers
and their weather obsession,
and when I laughed, I splattered peas and carrots
all over the tablecloth.

Mother was furious until
Mr. Griffin started laughing so hard at my mess
that he knocked over
the bowl of mashed potatoes.

Mother joined us then
with one of her deep belly laughs,
and we all ate our spuds
off the table.

After pie à la mode, I beat him
in chess, Parcheesi, and Old Maid.
Mother sent me up early with a look that said
"Don't argue," and for once, I didn't.

I wasn't sleepy, though, so I tiptoed
to the roof and stretched out under the stars.
Through the window below,
that new love tune "Blue Moon"
drifted up from the radio.

LOSING

My grown-up self
keeps arguing with my childish self
about how much happiness
Mother should have—

I guess I just never imagined
she'd need more than me and Uncle Jeff,
but I guess
she does.

Then Mike mentions his aunt from Indiana
coming out here to set things right
and maybe he'll have to leave town for a while.
I know I should be wanting what's best for Mike.

I know I should be feeling like
I'm gaining a father,
but it feels more like
I'm losing my mother.

SCRAPBOOK ENTRY

Federal agents cornered
Ma Barker and her son Freddie
in their hideout
in Oklawaha, Florida.

Ma believed crime
was a family business
and schooled her four sons
to be kidnappers, killers, and thieves.

Together they robbed local banks
of over one million dollars,
kidnapped three people,
and murdered ten.

But every Sunday
Ma dragged Freddie, Doc, Herman, and Lloyd
off to church
to sing and to pray.

Now Ma and Freddie are dead
and all the bank tellers and ministers in Florida
are sleeping a little bit
easier.

REASONABLE DOUBT

The laws of New Jersey say
that if a murder is committed
during an attempted burglary,
then it is murder in the first degree,
even though no harm
was intended.

(That's fair, I suppose—
if someone dies, they are dead
whether the killing was intentional
or not.)

The laws of New Jersey say
that first-degree murder is punishable
by death.
Death by electric shock.
Death in the electric chair.

If the jury believes that Bruno Richard Hauptmann
broke into the Lindberghs' house,
intending to steal their child
(or even just the clothing the child was wearing)
and the child died,
then Bruno Richard Hauptmann is guilty
of first-degree murder.

If, however, there is "reasonable doubt"
about the evidence presented against him
(the ladder, the ransom money, the handwritten notes,
or the witnesses' testimony),
then he should be
acquitted.

On the last day of the trial,
Judge Trenchard explained all this to the jury,
who listened carefully
while I wrote down every word.

Now it is up to those twelve
to decide
if Bruno Richard Hauptmann made that ladder,
or, if he didn't,
if he wrote those ransom notes,
or, if he didn't,
if he was lurking in the bushes on March 1, 1932,
or, if he wasn't,
if he called out "Hey, Doctor!"
late at night in a New York cemetery,
or, if he didn't,
if he lifted the Lindbergh baby out of his crib
and dropped him
while he carried him down the ladder
and later buried him,
or, if he didn't.

I watch the twelve walk out of the room
in single file.

I watch Bruno Richard Hauptmann walk out of the room
between two armed guards.
They all look tired.
They are all sick of this trial.
They all just want
to go home.

DELIBERATION

Uncle Jeff paces back and forth
across the newsroom floor, occasionally
scratching at his cast,
waiting.

Mother rushes back and forth
across the hotel dining room,
seating customers and clearing tables,
waiting.

I ride my bicycle up and down
Cemetery Hill until it's dark,
then I make snow angels behind the courthouse
near the gazebo in the park,
waiting.

At ten o'clock, the whole town—
nearly everyone who lives here—
and all who have come from somewhere else to see the trial
(about seven thousand, the newspapers say)
crowd around the courthouse,
waiting.

At 10:27, the bell atop the courthouse
begins to ring, someone
begins to shout "Kill Hauptmann! Kill Hauptmann!"
and almost the whole town
joins in.

VERDICT

My press badge lets me get in at the back.
The courtroom is packed and smells
like damp wool and dirty socks.

It has taken twelve people eleven hours
to decide the fate
of Bruno Richard Hauptmann.

Judge Trenchard asks: "What say you?
Do you find the defendant
guilty or not guilty?"

The jury foreman replies: "Your honor,
we find him guilty
of murder in the first degree."

Judge Trenchard pronounces the death sentence
as Bruno Richard Hauptmann,
with sunken eyes and ashen complexion,

looks around in disbelief.
Head down, Anna, his wife,
sobs silently.

Part V

"I dreaded this assignment more than any other . . .
I wondered whether justice would be served
by snuffing out the life of this man."

—Robert Elliot, executioner

"HAUPTMANN . . . REMAINS SILENT TO THE END"

—*The New York Times* headline, April 4, 1936,
the morning after Hauptmann's execution

LETTER FROM A FRIEND

I got a letter from Indiana.
The first part said:

Dear Katie,

This new place is pretty nice.
Aunt Jo gave me my own room, and Uncle Ed
fixed up his bike so I can ride back and forth
to town. My new school is smaller than the one
in Flemington, but they have a good baseball team
and I'm fixing to try out for left field.

The second part was written
in different ink,
like he had walked away
and come back later.

There are no trains, though, and no one
I can really talk to
if I really need to talk.
My dad is trying to get well in a hospital
fifty miles from here, so
I'm not sure when I'll be back.

Do you still go there?
(The tracks, I mean.)
I hope you do.

I'm putting a postcard in this envelope
so you'll know what Indiana looks like.
If you want to, you can write me back.
                    Your friend,
                    Mike

VIEW FROM THE HILL

I've been sitting up here for hours,
trying to make some sense
out of everything that's happened:
My town was invaded by Hollywood and the press,
Mike has left, and Uncle Jeff
has become my best friend;
my mother's dating the *Democrat* editor,
and Bruno Richard Hauptmann has been sentenced
to death.

Some days I feel almost normal,
but others it's like I'm riding a circus carousel
and every time I reach out to grab that brass ring
someone else yanks it away
and I just keep
spinning and spinning and spinning.

I'm tired of my scrapbook.
I haven't gone down to the tracks.

Up here, everything used to lay out so neatly,
everything seemed
pretty clear and straight.
Now all the streets run slantwise
and even the steeples look crooked.

If Mike were here, he'd say
I'm just waking up to how it is,
and maybe he'd be right.

I hope I start feeling better
about how it is
real soon.

THE TROUBLE WITH
SMALL TOWNS

is that you can't
disappear.

Every time I think I'm settled into some
inconspicuous space
where no one can find me for a while
and I'm all set to get
real still and quiet and let
faces and scenes from the trial
drift through my mind,
or maybe I just need to work out a problem
for an hour or so on my own—

whenever I find a place like that,
someone always seems to find
me.

Last weekend, for example, I had just
curled up with a copy of the *Saturday Evening Post*
in a corner of the *Democrat* attic
between the stacks of back issues and a few
spare parts for the printing press
when Mr. Griffin came in with his portable light
and turned white as a ghost when he saw me.
"What the heck—?? Katie Leigh . . .What on earth?"

And I told him the world was just
too darn crowded and loud, and where's
a girl like me supposed to go when she
needs a few minutes to herself?

On Monday, Mr. Griffin gave me
a sign he'd made—"KEEP OUT! INVENTORY IN PROGRESS"—
and said I could hang it on the attic door
anytime.
I think Mr. Griffin is softer
on the inside than he looks
on the outside,
and I think I'm learning
to like him.

PROMISE

"I'm not going to do anything that will
ruin our family—it was you and me first,
and that's the way it'll stay
unless we both want it different."

That's what Mother said
after supper
when we were standing at the sink
washing dishes.

I stopped my drying
and looked at her the same way
she looked at me
when I first told her I wanted to be
a reporter.

"Maureen Kathryn Flynn, I believe you," I said.

THIN LINE

I taped Mike's postcard to my closet.
Indiana looks sunny and
flat.

For the first time in a while, I went
down to the tracks.
On the way, I stopped in at the *Democrat*
to see Mr. G. and to tell him
I'd like to beat him at Parcheesi
anytime he's free.

Mother's birthday is on Sunday, and I'm buying
two train tickets to New York
so she and Mr. G.
can see a show.

Even so, there's still a little left in the Vacation Fund,
and I'm thinking I'll put it in
the coffeepot for my future
after all.

Funny how I'm not
so sure of things anymore—
like if I still want to be a reporter,
like if I want Mr. Griffin to be my father,
like if I'll keep writing to Mike
and how I'll feel when he comes home.

Maybe someday
I'll look back on this winter
and write down everything I can remember.
Maybe I'll be a novelist
or a photographer.

For now, I'm just going to take it slowly,
sit at the tracks,
watch the train men turn the engine,
watch the boxcars unhitch and recouple,
watch the forklifts load the flatbeds
and the fireman shovel coal,
until the last train leaves
and all I can see
is that thin line of steam.

EPILOGUE

"They think when I die, the case will die.
They think it will be like a book I close.
But the book, it will never close."

—Bruno Richard Hauptmann

After the trial ended on February 13, 1935, Flemington, New Jersey, returned to its quieter, pretrial state. The reporters and radio hosts went back to their respective cities, and the celebrities returned to Hollywood or New York. But the outcome of the Lindbergh case remained a topic of fierce debate. In a prominent article published the following day, the *New York Times* said: "The long trial at Flemington . . . and the verdict of the jury [have] established a crime, but did not clear away a mystery."

The fact remained that no one had actually *seen* who climbed the wooden ladder and entered the second-floor window of the Lindberghs' home, nor had anyone witnessed the killing (accidental or intentional) of their baby. The fact remained too that several of the witnesses' stories had changed drastically in the months between their first police interviews and their final courtroom testimonies. In the weeks following the verdict, many well-respected lawyers, writers, and politicians made public their doubts about the fairness of the trial. The President's wife, Eleanor Roosevelt, was among them: "[It] . . . left me with a question in my mind. . . . I can't help wondering what would happen if it were an innocent person on trial."

The newly elected governor of New Jersey, Harold Hoffman, added his own voice to those who felt that the unprecedented media coverage and the mishandling of witnesses and evidence by the police had made a fair trial impossible. He decided to reopen the case and allow the defense (now consisting of three local lawyers—Reilly had been fired) to bring forth any new evidence in its appeals to the higher courts.

The police believed that Hauptmann, under the strain of interrogations, imprisonment, and the trial, would eventually confess to the kidnapping. But Hauptmann did not confess. If anything, his pleas of innocence grew stronger as his execution drew nearer. Even when a New York editor offered him $90,000 (enough to secure the future of his wife and son) for a confidential confession to be published after his execution, Hauptmann refused. Hauptmann's devotion to his family was evident throughout the trial, so his refusal of such a huge sum threw an even darker shadow over the verdict.

In the next twelve months, the defense lawyers made four appeals to various courts of law. All four were rejected, mostly because no substantial new evidence was found that would place the blame for the kidnapping on anyone else. In Hauptmann's words: "[A] poor child has been kidnapped and murdered, so somebody must die for it. For is the parent not the great flier? And if somebody does not die for the death of the child, then always the police [and the attorneys and witnesses] will be [fools]. So I am the one who is picked to die."

Twice, when it seemed that new information might clear Hauptmann's name, the governor delayed his execution. But in the end, he could not prevent it. At 8:41 P.M. on April 3, 1936, the accused man was strapped into the electric chair and fitted with a black mask. Fifty-seven witnesses, including many journalists and policemen, sat across from him, waiting in silence. At exactly 8:44 P.M., the executioner pulled the switch. At 8:47 P.M., Bruno Richard Hauptmann was declared dead. One of the defense lawyers who had befriended him read Hauptmann's written statement:

> I am glad that my life in a world that has not understood me has ended. Soon I will be at home with my Lord, so I am dying an innocent man. Should, however, my death serve for the purpose of abolishing capital punishment—such a punishment being arrived at only by circumstantial evidence—I feel that my death has not been in vain.

It is a sad irony that the same fame-seeking media that eroded Charles Lindbergh's privacy, put his family in jeopardy, and perhaps indirectly encouraged the baby's kidnapping also made it impossible to conduct the Flemington trial without prejudice or bias. Even those who felt Hauptmann was innocent had nothing but sympathy for the young, grief-stricken parents. The Lindberghs suffered enormously because of their son's kidnapping and death, and again during the subsequent investigation and trial. Once the verdict was announced, they hoped to heal their family in solitude.

But the American public's appetite for news and its obsession with celebrities did not dwindle. The Lindberghs continued to be plagued by reporters and photographers wherever they went. In addition, they began receiving death threats directed toward their second son, Jon.

Disgusted by their lack of privacy and fearful of another kidnapping, they fled to England in December 1935. There they lived a comparatively peaceful life for several years before returning to the United States. In addition to Jon, the couple had four more children: two girls and two boys.

Charles Lindbergh died on August 26, 1974, at the age of 72. He remained convinced, to the end of his life, that Hauptmann was guilty.

Lead defense attorney Edward Reilly entered a psychiatric hospital in 1937 and stayed for fourteen months. He died of a stroke in 1940.

After her husband's execution, Anna Hauptmann moved with her small son to the outskirts of Philadelphia, where she worked as a cleaning lady and a waitress in a pastry shop. She never changed her name, nor did she remarry. On January 10, 1992, she appeared on the news program *A Current Affair*. On national television, she repeated her claim that her husband was home with her on the night the Lindbergh baby was kidnapped, and that he knew nothing about the crime.

Until her death at the age of 95, on October 10, 1994 (on what would have been her sixty-ninth wedding anniversary), she continued to proclaim her husband's innocence.

Author's Note

In writing *The Trial,* I relied heavily on my memories of growing up in Flemington during the 1960s and 1970s. Many of the churches, streets, parks, and businesses mentioned in the book are real places that I frequented on foot or on my bicycle. My walks to and from school led me past the courthouse and jail where Hauptmann was held, tried, and condemned to death in February 1935. My grandmother, who was in high school then, recalls pressing her face against the courthouse window, trying to get a glimpse inside.

The Lindbergh kidnapping and the trial of Bruno Richard Hauptmann has fascinated me—and haunted me—for years. But it wasn't until I read A. Scott Berg's 1998 biography of Charles Lindbergh and saw the splendid musical play *Baby Case* at the Arden Theatre in Philadelphia that I began to consider writing about it. In conducting research, I read dozens of books about the Lindbergh family, the kidnapping, the investigation and trial, and the theories that have evolved about the crime. I watched the HBO movie *Crime of the Century,* based on Ludovic Kennedy's book of the same title, and returned to Flemington for one of the annual trial reenactments at the courthouse.

Ralph Waldo Emerson once said, "There is properly no history; only biography," and I tend to agree. The characters in my story— both real and imagined—are ordinary people who are working, loving, and struggling in a certain place, at a certain time, just as we are today. The particular historical context of their lives affects their behavior and their decisions, just as surely as our current situation affects our own. The economic realities of the Great Depression, the rise of the mass media, the country's fear of war and need for emotional escape, all combined to make the Flemington trial, unlike any before it, a true national spectacle.

Because the investigation of the kidnapping was carried out in the mid-1930s, without the benefit of modern forensics, certain aspects of the crime remain a mystery. But even more than the "facts" presented here, it is my hope that *The Trial* will be a starting point for readers to consider the complexities of human behavior, both individual and social, and to clarify their own concepts of truth and justice.

J.B.

Acknowledgments

My deepest gratitude to the following individuals and organizations whose assistance and encouragement made this book possible:

Mark Falzini, archivist at the New Jersey State Police Museum, who shared his extensive knowledge of the Lindbergh kidnapping, investigation, and trial. I am ever grateful for his help with the trial transcripts and other documents related to the case, and for his careful proofreading of the manuscript.

Harry Kazman, my former high school teacher, who produces and directs the annual trial reenactment at the Flemington courthouse. He provided me with a unique opportunity to put myself, quite literally, in Katie Leigh's place, and to witness firsthand the social dynamics of the courtroom.

The online trial archives of the *Hunterdon County Democrat,* which helped me keep track of all the players in this complicated tale. They also provided some useful anecdotes and details that promoted my understanding of the historical context of early 1935 and aided my shaping of a few of the story's characters.

A. Scott Berg's meticulously researched and well-written biography *Lindbergh,* which helped me to comprehend the Lindberghs as an extended family and to develop an empathy for the unimaginable stresses they endured. Berg's book, more than any other, underscored the extent to which the couple's privacy was continually compromised in order to feed an insatiable American press.

Ludovic Kennedy's book *Crime of the Century,* later made into an HBO original movie, which gave me an intimate look into the lives of Anna and Bruno Richard Hauptmann and the equally unimaginable anxieties they suffered in the course of Bruno's apprehension and trial. Kennedy also documents, in a most compelling way, the serious blunders made by law enforcement officials at every level in the course of their investigation.

The Newseum in Arlington, Virginia (soon to reopen in Washington, D.C.), where I spent a weekend immersed in media history. The museum's exhibits and its publications were instrumental to my understanding of the popular radio and newspaper figures of the 1930s, as well as their effect on the American public.

Michael Ogborn's musical play *Baby Case,* which I saw at the Arden Theatre in Philadelphia, helped me to understand the social climate of the 1930s and to visualize several of the key personalities in the media and in the Lindbergh household.

My friends Gwyn Oberholtzer and Susan Brennan, who patiently tolerated my early ramblings about the trial, my research, and my struggle to get started.

Eileen and Jerry Spinelli, who gave me the faith to write the book in the first place, encouraged me as I wrote it, provided invaluable feedback on early drafts, and introduced me to my editor. There are no words which adequately express my gratitude!

David Keplinger, a gifted poet and teacher, who taught me to listen to my poems and to trust that each one would find its form on the page. His steadfast mentoring and friendship served as a springboard to writing this book.

Joan Slattery, editor extraordinaire, who has made my first foray into historical fiction an enjoyable one. Her gracious and intelligent suggestions, and her patience with my many questions, allowed this manuscript to reach its full potential.

And finally, my family, Neil and Leigh Bryant, who tolerated the piles of books and papers that occupied a good portion of our house (and my car) as I wrote this story. They also read the early drafts and made several helpful comments. My love and thanks for their help and support.

J.B.

Jen Bryant has published poetry, picture books, and biographies. *The Trial* is her first novel for young readers. She grew up in Flemington, New Jersey, the same town where the Lindbergh kidnapping trial took place in 1935. A graduate of Gettysburg College, she lives in Pennsylvania.